Of Doomful Portent

Of Doomful Portent

Matthew M. Bartlett

Illustrations by Yves Tourigny

Gare Occult
2018

ISBN: 1985690934
ISBN-13: 978-1985690936

Layout by Robert Canipe, Third Lung Press

This one is for Larry – Matthew

This one is for my dad - Yves

Also by Matthew M. Bartlett

Happy Disease

Dead Air

Gateways to Abomination

The Witch-Cult in Western Massachusetts

Rangel

Creeping Waves

The Stay-Awake Men & Other Unstable Entities

The original version of Of Doomful Portent was an advent calendar with tear-away pages, published by Tallhat Press and designed and illustrated by Yves Tourigny. Praise for that edition:

"Matthew M. Bartlett has one of the most irrepressible, fiercely original voices in all of contemporary weird fiction. And no visual artist could complement (his) singular horrors more aptly than the remarkable Yves Tourigny, who outdid himself with the interior art and design of the book --inspiring, horrifying, hilarious, and unforgettable."
– Jon Padgett, author of *The Secret of Ventriloquism*

"Bartlett's vignettes scream through the static of an old-time radio that's metastasized to your skull. This labyrinthine stroll through hell barks out demon-trodden fables like a demented candy man selling razorblade-flavored sweets. You'll grin while they cut you and swallow them whole, such is the dark magic here. Bartlett has the ability to make the darkest horror sing like an angelic choir engulfed in flame, and you'll like what you hear." – Philip Fracassi, author of *Behold the Void*

"Bartlett doesn't disappoint in his latest offering of truly disturbing, mind-altering flash fiction. Get in the holiday spirit with 25 tales guaranteed to raise your blood pressure. These are the kind of nightmares that stay with you forever." - Max Booth III, author of *The Nightly Disease*

"Here is an advent calendar spat from Hell. This incendiary collaboration between Matthew M. Bartlett and Yves Tourigny -- two of the most dynamic talents in the business -- is black as pitch, and as funny as it is horrifying. Christmas in Leeds is coming; grab your favorite goat and join the revels under the weeping moon. Yes, you'll be sorry, but you'll dance like the devil first." – Nathan Ballingrud, author of *North American Lake Monsters* and *The Visible Filth*

"No one conjures nightmarish, disturbing literary imagery and situations more skillfully than does Matthew M. Bartlett, and I can't imagine an artist who could complement his visions more perfectly than Yves Tourigny does with his striking, ghastly illustrations. This little book is a gift to be savored at any time of the year." - Jeffrey Thomas, author of *Punktown*

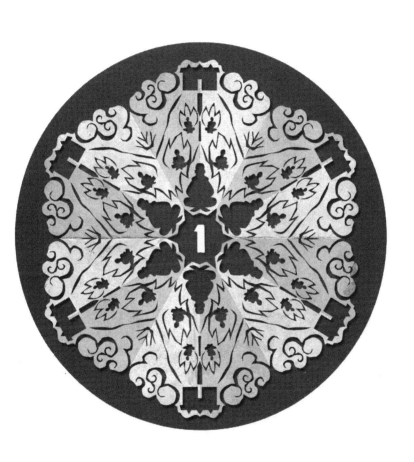

THE MANSE

The world ends every time a sentient being dies. Hundreds of thousands of apocalypses a day, piling up, metastasizing, a cancerous cloud that eats the world from the outside in and makes it clean.

A towering mansion on an expansive estate. Dusk. Tips of tree limbs poke out like charred fingers through the backdrop, a curved wall of fog. The long, broad front walk is lined with burning monks. I can just make out their blackening, hunched figures through the flames. The aromas fill the air. Frying skin, bubbling fat. My stomach whimpers with hunger. Inside, a party rages. Shadows flit and spin in the windows, they touch and separate. Glasses clink, music storms. The air vibrates with the screams of the guests.

A young man in a tuxedo runs out onto the porch and stumbles down the marble stairs, laughing wildly. A knife protrudes from his stomach, a steel pistil surrounded by petals of looped intestine. He falls on the bright green grass of the newly mown lawn, forcing the knife in deeper. The tip of the blade pushes at the back of his jacket. I kneel. He is lapping dew from the grass, his face a mask of sexual ecstasy. He humps weakly at the ground a few times, and then he dies. I flip him over, smooth his hair, push his eyelids down. They open again. He must want to see me. We regard one another. The world falls away.

After a time, I leave him be and enter the house. The party has ended, most of the guests dispersed. I find a partygoer curled up on the staircase, his bowtie undone, his cummerbund dangling, a champagne glass in his hand. I pry the glass from his fingers. Tipping it all the way up,

I drink what's left. Brackish pool water, tinged with algae and chlorine. Acrid. Foul. I spit it out.

A noise at the top of the stairs. Hovering at the landing is an old man, stout, skin blue-veined white marble. An elongated, deformed cranium. He is wearing only an orange diaper. He edges toward the top step, sideways, crab-like. I retreat and he tilts his head, his expression inscrutable. He opens his mouth and sings wordlessly. His voice is that of an angel. Piss bubbles at the lower edge of the diaper, then runs down his legs, over his dry, claw-like toes. It waterfalls down the staircase. I back away as the urine puddles at the foot of the stairs, darkening the marble floor as it expands. Swirls and curlicues of blood unfurl. The ammonia reek is overpowering.

I remove my shoes, let the warmth wash over my feet. Averting my gaze, I look up at the high ceiling, where a chandelier turns in lazy circles. It is crawling with bruised infants. Their silence is alarming. I don't want to see them fall. They clamber and grasp, little toes gripping the arms and the chains, little hands grabbing at the candle cups and columns. One does fall. I watch her face. I close my eyes when she lands, but the sound will stay with me always.

I hear sirens. Blue and red paint the walls.

The world ends each time a sentient being dies. Hundreds of thousands of extinctions a day, piling up, multiplying, a legion of tumors that disfigure the world.

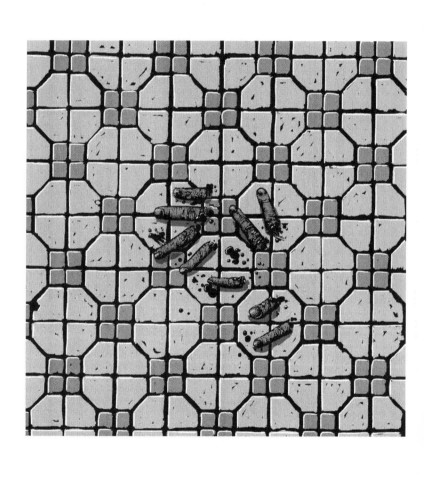

THE SIALOGOGUE – A TRANSMISSION

Drumming, far-away. Female voice loud, distorted: cobalt blue smoke.

Whispering male voice: *I keep seeing a stick-figure skinny man walking two dogs. He was on the corner of Main and Gothic Streets when someone walking by me said, "Those aren't dogs, you know." I looked carefully, then I saw, really saw, and I jammed my fist against my closed lips and hurried away as quickly as possible. Now I change my paths, use circuitous routes, avoid the places where I've seen the man walking the two things that are decidedly, horribly not dogs.*

Male voice: *Hey, Ariel, um, I'm making this call 'cause I want to tap to see if, um, I can, like, audio separator AUDIO, um, so, um, please don't put me on speakerphone, I just want only your voice to be heard.* (female voice cutting in and out: *lost my fingertips when I was little....never told me how...how I envied the girls ... painted nails...fear the long-fingered men...). That's exactly what I'm going to use if you say anything, um, and I'm almost at thirty seconds and that should be enough. Okay? Alright? Bye?*

Audience laughter, applause.

Male voice: *No, no. No. Ha ha. Seriously. I let it live under my tongue. It nourishes itself there and grows stronger. Would you like to see?* Audience roars its approval. One voice rises above the others, that of a woman. *Let me out, please. This was a mistake. This is all for me. He's doing this to get back at me. And you people paid money to see it. Please just...let go of my arm. Get away. Get away.* Cacophony, the audience roar swells like a cloud of startled birds. Female voice, loud, distorted: *... the red-windowed charnel houses on Fruit Street...*

Male voice: *I push my thumbnail up under the curl of my upper lip until I find a fault line, a separation.*

I dig upward, using the untrimmed nail as a knife. I squeeze the lip between my thumb and forefinger and peel upward, tearing skin from muscle. The sink grows pink, the light red. The air screams from the vent. I am a horror in red and black streaks. I know now that the things my supervisor said, those clichés and business-speak banalities, were in fact ancient incantations, older than religion, pre-speech. Serrated, broken blades burst from my hands. My dead fingers scatter across the blue and white tiles, just genetic code, ones and zeroes, human debris.

Female voice: *You have reached the Leeds Civic Association, meetings are by appointment only... continue being reached press one. I'm sorry. Shaky today. *unintelligible* in the refrigerator, I think. I tied it up.* Synthesized voice: *Please hold. Your call has been disconnected due to communication problems. Please stay on the line. (faint) have reached* (drumming, far away) Male voice: *Yeah?* Different female voice: *Hello?*

ME, MY UNSELF, AND I

The red and white stripes swirl. The magazines sit splayed across the waiting room table, their address labels stripped. In the corner the idiot television babbles inanities. The barber's scissors fly about the jug-eared head that juts from the hair-covered cape. On the tip of the barber's fat nose, reading glasses perch, smudged like the windows of an abandoned house. He squints, his lips moving to some unknown song. Then the lips stop. The bottom lip trembles. He begins to weep. It is an ugly sound, made uglier by his attempts to repress his wails. His left hand covers his mouth.

"No," says the head atop the cape. "That's too short. Too short, Mister. What have you done. What have you done. What's wrong with you? A man asks for a trim."

"A trim. What man asks for a trim?"

"Just a trim, I said. I said just a trim. A man…"

"A man gets a haircut. No trim. A trim is a mirror of another man's work. I'm good at what I do. Let me work. You will like it."

"…asks for a trim, he wants a trim. Look at this." The man points his nose at the clumps of hair all down the cape. The barber lunges forward, grabs a clump, retreats through the curtains at the back of the shop.

"Where is he going now?" the man says to the empty barber shop. A woman on the television cackles helplessly.

The barber returns with an oblong box. He sweeps his arm along the small counter below the mirror, sending to the floor his scissors and combs and his spray bottles. He puts the man's hair into the box. Then he tilts the box forward so the man can see.

The box is full of hair. Blonde hair, grey hair, brown and red. Curly and straight. A voice comes from the hair, a tinny, wavering note. A small hand of woven hair rises from the box, the size of a doll's hand. The thing crawls out. Black eyes open in its head, shining.

The man struggles under the cape. His hand pops out alongside his neck, squeezes past his ear, a cigarette lighter held between his thumb and his palm. The cape falls around the man's shoulder.

The barber bats at the man's hand, but to no avail. The man thrusts the lighter forward. The hair-man catches on fire. It shrieks. Both men cover their ears. The flame burns hot and fast, a stream of smoke pouring up to the ceiling and spreading across it like ink. The walls crumple and the mirrors shatter, showering the men with glass. The barber retreats to the corner, bawling. The buttons pop off of the cash register one after the other, shooting like bullets up through the ceiling tiles. The magazines fly into the thickening smoke and flap and flutter about like winged things. Hair clippings and smoke fill the shop. The scissors launch from the floor and embed themselves into the customer's throat. He stumbles around, waving his arms, batting away the magazines and the hair. Blood shoots from his neck in long, bright red projectiles. The hair man, dying, sings a terrible song. The barber joins in. The man joins the duet, whistling through the hole in his throat. The town siren joins the chorus. Night falls on this mad, fiery death dirge in the barber shop next to the convenience store as the world rushes by outside unknowing.

TEUFELSKAPPE

My therapist, Doctor Rittle, sails into the room like a fat white apparition and falls backward just where an easy chair happens to be; his raspy sigh and its yelp of complaint form a short, sad duet. During our sessions, the doctor speaks solely in anagrams and, occasionally, comes out with that linguistic rarity known as the anagrammatic palindrome.

I happened to see him downtown today, hovering outside the lingerie store. He cuts an unmistakably enigmatic figure: the long coat that trails behind him on the walk, two pairs of glasses on chains around his frog-like neck, the bald head, the broom-ends of hairs spilling from his preternaturally large ears, and the cane, which looks like the long, gnarled bone of some impossible animal.

When he spotted me, he grinned a guilty grin, revealing that horrible black tooth, in spite of the fact (or, more worrying, *because of* the fact) that he knows it unsettles me so.

Now, he sits, fingers intertwined under his chin. He is silent today, which means that I must start the session on my own. I'm onto his ruses.

He expects a statement.

I offer a question.

"Doctor," I say. What is fear?"

His cheeks crease and split horizontally, his lower face rupturing and separating into a constellation of insectile mandibles and black needle-teeth. A long, purple-veined tongue unfurls and crushes the glass of water on the arm of his chair. Water, ice, and glass spread over the surface of the arm and splash onto the floor. Doctor Rittle uses his sleeve to dry his dampened brow. His face settles, reconstitutes itself into a semblance of human features.

"Well, fear redefines itself fluidly throughout our

lifetimes," he begins.

NIGHTEYES

Norman Jericho, shoeless, in a blue and white bathing suit, walks slowly along the beach, pushing his toes into the wet sand. His belly hangs over the waist of the bathing suit. He shivers. The waves try in vain to shush the town. The lights of the houses and the shops twinkle. Parties rage and roar. Out of the half-light emerges a man in a suit. He is an older man. His white hair flies about his head. The man veers in Norman's direction, blocking his path. When they are face to face, Norman sees that the old man has two eyes in each socket, green eyes, pushed up against one another.

I see, said the blind man.

And he picked up his hammer and saw.

The old man reaches up with a liver-spotted hand and pulls his jaw from his head. His skin and muscles stretch and snap like chewing gum. His tongue flops down like a pink, wet, bifurcated necktie. He proffers the jaw to Norman. Norman, ever polite, accepts it. The old man walks into the sea. Norman watches him go. After a time, just the man's head bobs in the water. The water covers his ears. Then just the disk of the top of the man's head, then he is gone.

Norman sits in the sand, holds the jaw out, tips it this way and that. He runs the tip of his index finger along the top of the uneven row of teeth.

-Aren't you cold?

It's a little cold.

-Do you know Mr. White Noise?

The old man who walked into the water?

-Oh, no. Mr. White Noise is much older than that man. He is that which lies beyond annihilation. Unceasing agony, sentient rot. His is a song long ago sung whose echo still resounds. But not forever, Norman. Soon the echo will fade and the party will begin. The sign of Mr.

White Noise resides here.

Resides where?

-Right here, Norman.

Norman turns the jaw so that the teeth face away from him. With the fingernails of his thumb and his forefinger he scrapes the tender epithelium of the floor of the jaw, slicing at glands, rupturing ducts. Blood wells up, stains his fingernails. He catches the edge of something hard, pulls it out. It is a coin. The incoming tide has reached him now, pools under his feet. He rinses the coin in the ocean water. On its face is something like a 4 and something like a capital A. On the reverse side is the image of a man whose face is ringed with eyes. The coin grows hot in his hand and he drops it.

It is night now. Something is coming up from the ocean. Heads bobbing out past the breakers. Their shoulders breach the surface. They are silhouetted. Norman cannot make out their features.

Somewhere behind him, on the houses that climb the cliff faces, the sounds of glass breaking, terrible shrieks, roaring laughter, breaking bones. He turns and flees the ocean. All the windows in all the houses are lit. As the things attain the shore, Norman flees into the tall grasses and hides. The sand claims the coin. The men from the sea claim the town. The echo fades.

I see, said the blind man.

And he picked up his hammer and saw.

THE END OF THE FAMILY LINE

I should have known when I saw the unfamiliar man among the mourners. I at first took him for one of the drivers. A new hire, I said to myself, for I happen to have as my very close friend Mr. Lawrence Stoneblack, the founder of Leeds Livery De-Luxe, and I know the drivers to a man. The stranger stood by the great old oak at the center of the cemetery, consulting his phone, eyes masked by mirrored glasses that reflected the mourners in distorted miniature. He pocketed the phone and pulled from his concealed holster a .45. He took the lives of my Aunt Rosacea and my dear cousin Wilhelm before I opened his throat with my Chinese throwing star.

Four days later at Wilhelm's funeral a man wound his car around the stones and the mausoleums and detonated the vehicle within yards of the family. Instantly killed by the shrapnel were my sister Ringette and her dachshund Willoughby. My cousin Brickfort was cut nearly in two by a piece of the Buick's hood, and died in hospital not long after. I lost one eye in the conflagration.

At Willoughby's wake, a twisted-up paraplegic in a wheelchair sprayed the mourners with gunfire from an AR-15 she'd secreted under a blanket on her lap. Sent into sulfer-scented oblivion were my Great Uncle Godfrey and my cousins Ansel, Gregor, Alfonse, and Roger.

I took a bullet to the collarbone and three to the gut. Here in my hospital bed I hold at my side a hand grenade said to be blessed by Mr. White Noise himself. When my remaining family arrives in one short hour, I will pull the pin, thus sparing them the pain of watching my slow deterioration and eventual death. In doing so, I will also stymie further attackers, as this is the last of the Boyle-Grassleys, and there will be no one left to mourn.

Hallelujah. Amen. I see, said the blind man.

Accerima proximorum odia.

Abiit nemine salutato.

.

IT WAS A TURKEY

Two emaciated but tautly muscled jackals were thrashing wildly on the walk in front of my house, vying for a wild turkey. The turkey, stripped of its feathers, screeched and screamed as the fangs and claws tore at its flesh. The jackals growled and snarled and barked. Wanting the noise to stop, I barged out of the house, grabbed two large metal garbage can lids from the porch, and began clanging them together. The jackals stopped and stared at me, letting the turkey spill to the pavement. Their eyes were rheumy, yellow, wild…eager. I backed slowly up the porch stairs, watching them watch me. They were crouched, lean coils of potential energy. I closed the door and they resumed their attack on the dying creature. The sounds recommenced, and an hour later they stopped.

I went outside with a shovel and, gagging and gasping, pushed together the scattered remains of the turkey. Then I buried it in the yard, ever watchful of the tree-line, wary of the distance between me and the safety of the house. A wind kicked up the dead leaves. The sun ducked behind the trees. A flurry began, little curled up spiders of snow meandering down from the dusk-blue sky. When the work was done, I went inside and stared for a while at the pages of a book until I drifted into sleep.

Now, waking, I choose to remember that it was a turkey. It was a turkey, please. A turkey.

WHAT KIND OF BODIES GO WITH RED

Mr. White Noise looked at Margaret through the cloud of smoke that still hung in the air after her heroically long exhalation. "But I've already said too much," he said. Margaret was perplexed. He hadn't said anything. Anything at all. Slowly she raised a slender, elegant fist into the smoke cloud and extended a pinky finger like it was a small ballet dancer unfurling on a stage all but obscured by theatrical fog.

Mr. White Noise grinned a greedy grin. Quick like a frog he shot out his tongue, long, barbed like that of a cat. It wrapped around the finger and pulled, stripping it to the bone. The tongue retreated into his mouth. He chewed vigorously and Margaret crumpled to the floor, holding her wounded left hand in her right. She looked up at him.

She held up her right hand, extended her pinky finger. "Again," she said.

"I'm full," he replied, and he licked his lips with a black and cracked tongue.

They sat on opposite ends of the sectional in the fire-lit living room, smoking. The fire threw strange shadows around the place. Margaret had taped a fat, bloodied bandage around her pinky finger. Mr. White Noise's eyes showed only whites, shot through with a web of red veins. He talked backwards, the impenetrable monologue punctuated by backwards laughter, helpless and warped, like the chuckling of some idiot giant. Margaret's uninjured hand played under her tights and she lifted her legs in the air, toes clenched. Her eyelids began to flutter.

The doorbell rang.

"Goddammit, you ruined it," Margaret said through clenched teeth. She pulled out her hand and smelled it, her eyes squeezed shut, and then wiped it on the cushion, leaving a dark red smear. Then she rose and went to get the door. Mr. White Noise's monologue trailed off into a funereal, wavering hum. His fingers danced in the air.

The slender, grey thing with the long fingers and the too-heavy head limped into the room and flung onto the carpet two small, grey bodies. They landed awkwardly, stiffened and dead. From one of their mouths came a clicking and a long, strange sound like a sigh. Mr. White Noise clapped his hands. His tongue went to work, stripping the bodies. Blood pooled on the carpet. Margaret backed up to the sideboard, keeping her eyes on the feeding. He had said he was full. She felt her ears grow hot, the flush of rejection spreading to her face and neck. With a shaking hand she poured herself a glass of wine. The wine roiled like a storm-shaken ocean in the glass. She drank greedily, then set the glass on the floor and leaned against the sideboard, threw her head back. "Oh," said Margaret. "Oh."

THE MEAL AT THE FERN DINER

The man struts onto the dancefloor. His cummerbund dangles at his side and his shirt is stained with blood and mud and mustard. His hair is unkempt, pushed up at the ears like great wings. His hands, thrust out straight, hold a Bakelite radio, yellow, with a black handle. On the front of the radio is painted a garish face. Dashed brown nostrils. Black rimmed eyes with green, amorphous eyeballs. A huge mouth with a splash of white in the middle to represent teeth. It's blaring its own music, leaping violins and funereal bass, aural graffiti smeared across the façade of the stately waltz of the house band, who continue to play undaunted.

People move away from the man. A stench wafts off of him: unwashed flesh, neglected excrement, the sharp and cruel tang of urine. His expression is…unseemly. A small but enthusiastic erection juts at his pants. Couples unclasp hands, release waists, peel off to the carpeted expanse of abandoned dinner tables. Coats are retrieved, furs donned. The door opens again and again, admitting gusts of frigid December air as the couples flee two-by-two. The man laughs as he twirls along under the red and blue and yellow lights. Now one hand holds the radio's side, the other caresses its face, comes away stained. The face is now a smeared horror. "My love," he says. "My love."

The radio whispers to him. He holds it to his ear. His eyes widen. He opens his mouth and vomit spills down the front of his shirt. He appears to not notice.

The Fern Diner. The man has placed the radio at the opposite edge of the table, facing him. In front of it sits a sad plate of strewn scrambled eggs and a crumpled potato. A wilted sprig of parsley hugs the edge of the plate. Before the man, split among two plates: a pile of thick-cut bacon; a stack of fat, golden pancakes; the sightless yellow eyes of a pair of pristine eggs; a bloody mountain of hash; a split English Muffin, crannies bearing oceans of bubbly butter; a piled stack of charred sausage links. Forming a half-circle around the plates: a carafe of orange juice and a small empty cup; a large glass of iced water; a cup of coffee black as the deep sea; ramekins of syrup, amber glinting under the soft diner lights.

A bald, white-clad waiter separates from a convocation of management and wait staff and approaches the table. His fists are clenched. The wind outside, sensing confrontation, howls in protest. A few pale and despondent men clad only in pajamas stagger down the thoroughfare, or stand shivering in deep storefront doorways. The church's steeple retracts and its stained-glass windows rumble in their casements. The waiter reaches the table. He slams his fists onto the edge of the table, rattling the flatware, then grabs the radio and runs to the kitchen.

The unkempt man, screaming a raspy, high pitched scream, scrambles from his seat to give chase. The waiter hurls the radio into the fryer. The sounds of its disintegration are very loud. The unkempt man dives in after it.

The waiters sit in the capacious corner booth, crowded onto the round cushiony seats. They peel the clothing and skin from the man splayed on the table, and gnaw at the flesh underneath. Bones crack between their teeth. Blood and fat cake their mustaches. They chew and slurp and groan with unfettered pleasure. The radio, a lump of melted and charred plastic, sits next to the man. A woman sings mournfully from the crumpled speaker. She sings of hanged brides, of stillborn babies, of putrefaction and infanticide and bodies crushed under the wheels of mammoth trucks. She sings of split skulls and torn-open throats and diseases of the skin and the tongue. Her voice is the caress of dead flesh dragged across polished stone.

The owner watches from behind the circular window in the door that leads to the kitchen. His breaths come in little bursts. He is standing on a floor of raw ground meat. He curls and uncurls his toes. It makes him so very pleased to see his workers happy. He sings along with the radio as he slides the chef's knife back and forth across his exposed belly.

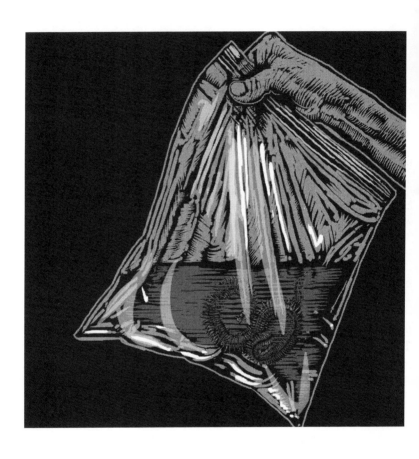

THE WILLING HOST

A seaside motel. The smell of a winter morning mingling with the salty aromas of beach junk and ocean salt. The woman opened the door in only a towel, her brown hair wet, her cheeks flushed. The short man said, "Are you of age? Let me see some I.D."

"All right. Geez, though. Hell of a way to introduce yourself."

She walked over to the desk and fished through her purse. The man looked at her pink feet, the pores on her smooth bare calves, the shape of her rump under the towel. His gaze lingered for a time, and then he looked around the room. There were two beds. One was made up, tucked in, neat as you please. On the other sat an open suitcase, jaw wrenched open as though it had choked to death from vomiting out clothing. The credenza was littered with detritus: empty soft drink bottles; snack food wrappers; a profusion of opened sandwich bags like translucent, slack-mouthed fish. The woman turned around, her license in her hand. She started to walk to him, but suddenly bent and barked out a series of loud, wracking, lung scarring coughs. She doubled over, put her hands on her knees as the coughing intensified. The smell of phlegm and blood, of stale tobacco, assaulted the man's nose. He went to her, plucked the license from her hand. 23 years old. An address in Leeds, Massachusetts, over a hundred miles to the west. In the picture she had longer, darker hair, too much makeup. He flicked the license to the floor, pulled off his jacket and threw it down at the foot of the bed. He kicked off his shoes and began to undo his pants.

The door slammed open behind him. Fear spread through his body as he turned. The man in the doorway was narrow and tall, with terrifying huge hands and a face far too large for his head. He grinned at the short man as

53

he ducked his head to enter. Then he grinned past the man at the woman.

"Maximilian," the woman said.

"Cassandra."

The short man ducked around him and fled into the cold, leaving his jacket and shoes behind.

Maximillian sat on the edge of the bed. A stack of stiff and virginal hundred dollar bills now stood among the sandwich bags. "What have you brought me?" he asked.

Cassandra, now in jeans and a faded t-shirt, dug the rest of her clothes out from the suitcase, pulled out a baggie. Something many legged and fat and purple-red wriggled around in dirt-dotted seawater. She opened the baggie. Maximillian pulled the thing out between his thumb and forefinger. "Watch," he said. "Don't turn away, and don't avert your eyes."

Cassandra watched. She didn't even blink. He liked that, she knew, so she'd trained herself to do it. Stinger-tipped stalks emerged from under the thing's blind eyes and attached themselves to the skin of his hand, dug in deep, blood bubbling up around them. He pulled it from his hand with his teeth, biting into it, hard. Blood splashed his face and neck as he forced it down his throat, his teeth sawing back and forth. Once he'd choked it down, he sucked the severed stingers from his hand, leaving gaping black holes ringed with a sickly orange slime.

"Ooh, baby," said Cassandra. "Good job. Listen…" Then she began to cough again, ferocious and raspy. She held up one finger as if to say *just a sec*. When she was done, she looked up through tear-streaked eyes. The whites of Maximillian's eyes had gone black, and his hands were in pieces and shreds on the bed. Skeleton fingers wriggled and crumpled like chalk.

He opened his mouth and screamed and screamed.

She got the knife out and plunged it into his throat. He

slid down from the bed, gargling. She dragged him down the beach to the ocean before that thing could get out of his body and into the room...if it hadn't already, while she was coughing. She grabbed the wallet from the back of his pants and left him in the waves. A couple walking hand in hand in winter coats watched her, mouths agape.

Back in the room, she counted her money. She whistled as she re-packed her bag. Under the bed, the thing grew and grew.

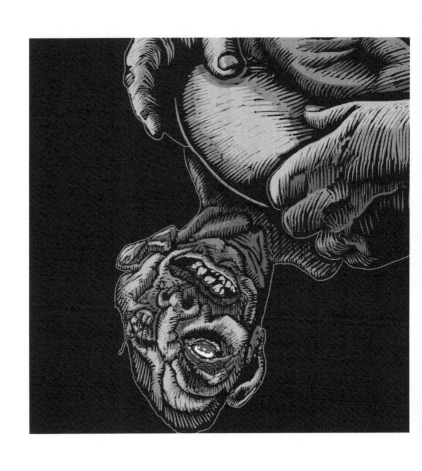

THE SUN IS A MINOR STAR

The unofficial name for the mute, ugly man who stood at the corner of Main and Gothic Streets was the Tumor Man, for his belly protruded from under his rib cage at a right angle, jutting out into the world like a dirty truth. He was constantly pulling up his pants, drooling long, shimmering brown tendrils. From his wretched person emanated the odors of sour sweat and dried saliva, old chocolate, gingivitis, excreta both ancient and new.

Also, rumors. He was unimaginably wealthy. He was Reginald Fourtier, the man responsible for much of the city's growth in the early 1970s, who had disappeared in 1980 and was now swollen, deformed - unrecognizable. He lorded over a harem of corpulent sex slaves susceptible to mind control. He was an avatar of Gaap, a powerful prince in Hell and servant of Amaymon. He was the nth reincarnation of the mad Pope St. Sevenius, eater of babies' hearts.

I gave no credence to those rumors. He was just a man, a fallen man, destroyed by chemicals, those inside him from birth, those self-administered, or a combination of the two. My wife often wondered aloud why none of the rumors addressed his grotesque abdominal protuberance.

It came as a surprise to me when I opened my front door, returning home after an interminable day doing the bidding of my capricious and cruel employers, to detect his unmistakable odor in my very house. I tracked it to the den, where the man befouled my couch, Ruby opposite him in my armchair, which she had moved from the corner.

The man's striped shirt had been hiked up to just above his sagging breasts. His fat, filthy hands held up the large flap of his belly, as if he was preparing to fold it like a bedsheet. The odor was overpowering. I gagged. But

59

I saw the true horror only once I had circled around to stand behind Ruby. From under the man's belly protruded a truncated torso and head, as though some hideous goblin had gotten stuck during a breach birth. The man looked down, staring at it, breathing ragged breaths.

The head was terribly deformed. One eyeball shone bright red, speckled with white, ringed with greenish mucous. Where the other eye should be was just a puckered hole, two wiry hairs dangling from it. The mouth was elongated to an alarming degree. Teeth like bleached, split wood stuck out here and there, A tongue, a chewed up thing like a dog's old toy, appeared, ran itself across the bleeding lips in a vain attempt to moisten them, an atavistic endeavor to be sure.

It began to speak. It spoke of the outer edges of the universe, where things far more hideous than deep sea creatures sailed madly through black abysses, of the ruin and decay slurping up universes. It talked of the universe as a great, bulging bowel. It said that the Segmented Man would rise from deep inside the earth to befoul the minds of the newly born. It called me by my name and told my deepest secret.

Tumor Man looked to me. "I'm sorry," he whispered. "Please cut it off. Cut if off. I don't care if I die. Throw it in the fire." Ruby cackled and was upon him. "Get the knife," she said, and I did. There in our living room, she cut off the man's head, not the one he had meant, I was certain. Blood splashed the sofa, pooled on the floor beneath it. The thing at the man's belly cackled and chortled, egging us on, now whooping, now howling. In the encroaching darkness of the evening, on a street near the center of Leeds, where mad things dwelt, we locked the doors and closed the blinds and gave ourselves over to Him.

PICTURES OF CHILDREN

The police photograph is singularly upsetting, though not as upsetting as the acts purportedly carried out by the man in the photograph, Glenn Lapid, a man I once called Friend. Newspaper accounts agree that when caught, he struggled and lashed out and groaned and drooled, denied his guilt, tried to pull away and flee. After begging for the security guard to let him go, he collapsed onto the carpet, nearly feral there among the clothing racks and the gape-mouthed shoppers and the red and green shrapnel of impending Christmas.

For surely the realization had hit him that he couldn't go back thirty seconds and undo the deed, that life as he'd known it was over. He knew the minute the gloved hand grabbed his wrist and wrested away his phone that his remaining years—and there would be many of them; the Lapids were of singularly hearty stock—would be nothing less than horror stacked upon horror, his psychic dermis pulled back with violence and his raw innards exposed to the sting of public scrutiny.

The photograph: that of a man with his future torn suddenly away, his mouth hanging open, his cheeks hollow. Under lank, unwashed hair his eyes evince such despair, such terror, that it's difficult to look at, and at the same time difficult to look away from. It's a man who has watched as the life drained out of him, a cadaver that lives, can still feel, but only pain. His decomposition is ongoing, but existential rather than physical.

His call surprised me greatly, for we hadn't spoken in many years.

"Bill," he said, when I answered.

"Glenn? Glenn, son, how are you holding up?"

A long sigh. "I might have known you saw it."

"Glenn, I…"

"Bill, you have to listen. It wasn't what they said. The

pictures…they weren't for me."

"Middle school, girls, Glenn."

"Bill," he said, and the tone in which he said it sort of froze me.

When we were younger men, Glenn and I had had an abiding interest in the occult. We had studied the lives and works of the Hilltown Ten, a coven of local witches that operated for an unknown number of decades straddling the nineteenth and twentieth centuries, and we recreated (as best as we could, gleaning bits and pieces from the faded and expurgated tomes that documented their reign) some of their more notorious rituals and blood rites. The far off borders that they had brazenly breached we left alone, preferring to stay as much as possible within the confines of human decency and, of course, away from the steely clutches of the law.

As far as I could recall, Glenn had shed and disavowed this avocation, just as he'd done with the other vices and destructive habits that characterized his (and to a stronger degree *my*) younger years.

His voice told me that his perverted misadventure, truncated as it was by the exertions of the local police force, was not related to any kind of *urges* of Glenn's, but to something larger and more, let's say, organized.

"Bill," he said again, and his voice sank to a whisper. "I did it for the old men in the woods."

Then he cackled. "I know how it sounds, but it's true. The group is still operating, Bill. Today. As we speak. They're becoming more selective, do you see?"

"I see, Glenn. And you were acting on their behalf?"

"That's not *me*, Bill."

"What did you tell the police? What do you plan to tell them?"

I listened to him talk. He could not suffer the eternal desecration of his reputation and his character. Better to be thought insane or delusional than a pervert. And so on. I nodded, and at the end of the call I offered a few words of encouragement and understanding.

I hung up. Breathed. I offered up a prayer to the monstrous appetites of Pope Sevenius and knelt before the grotesque image of Abrecan Geist that spanned the wall of my den.

I made myself a drink, one part bourbon, one part blood. And then I stood, put on my coat, and went into the woods.

GENERALLY ACCEPTED ACCOUNTING PRINCIPLES, OR THE PIG OF THE RITUAL DREAM

Rat Knudsen sat on the edge of his chair, his fingers flying about the keyboard. To the right of the mousepad sat a cup of coffee cooling under a film of powdered creamer, the fanged, black-lipped mouth of a staple remover, a ball of rubber bands, and the severed head of a hog, swollen-eyed, a crust of snot at its nose, shit staining the edges of its ears, tongue out and split like the tongue of a serpent.

Donald entered the office and stopped cold. "Jesus, Kundsen, what in the holy hell?"

"Just a minute," said Rat, still typing furiously. The phone trilled thirteen times and fell quiet. The flies hummed with a lusty ardor.

"Do you want me to get you an apple for that thing's mouth? I have one in the fridge, if Nancy didn't steal it."

"Just a minute," said Rat.

"You have to get that thing out of here! Nicole will have your ass."

"Just a *minute*," said Rat.

Five minutes later he stopped typing and clicked 'save.'

Without turning, he said, "Got some news for you, Donny. You're not going to like it."

"What's up, Knudsen?"

"They're going to run you out on a rail."

"What?"

Knudsen spun around in his chair. He had been bleeding from both nostrils. The blood on his shirt looked like serrated suspenders. "First, they're going to start piling on responsibilities. They'll take jobs that have been split among the thirteen people in the department, and give them all to you. Some of the tasks will be so simple they could be done by a child. Others, epic in their impossibility, designed deliberately to obfuscate and confuse: a litany of exceptions whose rules remain a closely guarded secret.

"Then the meetings will start, just you and your management team. Furrowed brows. Tapping on notebooks. You'll tell them you're overloaded. They'll scoff. You'll ask for assistance. They'll say they'll see what they can do even as they pile on more and more.

"You've been here a long time, gotten a lot of raises. You make too much money for your position. They can't have that. And they can't countenance your getting any kind of severance."

Donald reached up and scratched his head with both hands. "This can't happen now, Ratty. The house…we'll be cutting back as it is."

Rat Knudsen smiled. He stood, picked up the hog's head. He held it up in the air, began spinning it around between his hands. He was whispering. Donald moved closer, closer, until he and Rat were nearly nose to nose. He listened. And began to smile.

Rat lowered the hog's head over Donald's.

FATHER LIGHT

There's some things you don't joke about," Raymond said.

Derek snorted. "Christ, Ray-Ray, do you even hear yourself? You sound like a prissy old grandma with your finger-wagging."

"Well, I'm sorry, but that's blasphemy."

Now Derek was doubled over, holding his sides. "You're worried about blasphemy, why'd you even come with me?"

"I wanted to see."

"Yeah, you wanted to see. Now you're sitting there with your eyes covered."

The boys, both thirteen years old, having each snuck from their respective houses in town, sat on the third step up from the floor, just below the altar in the Devil Church. It was nearly 3 a.m. The diabolical Church had acquired the venerable old building, formerly a Catholic church, an historic landmark, which the diocese had closed, the appeals of the faithful having been swiftly and summarily denied by the Apostolic Signatura of the Vatican.

At best, the earnest, disenfranchised parishioners said to each other at their fervent little meetings in the back room of the Bluebonnet Diner, the building might have been inhabited by a museum, a clinic. Worse, a dance hall that might host raves and concerts featuring music that did not countenance the glory of God, or even dared countermand Him. Worse than that, a "Gentleman's Club," the irony of that appellation nearly too rich to even countenance. They hadn't even dared speculate that the building might host worshipers of the Father of Lies, the Adversary.

Derek flicked his lighter. "Open your eyes," he said.

Ray opened his eyes briefly, saw the things swimming up and down the walls in the flickering light, saw the obscenities in the stained glass grapple with each other among red serpents, pink worms, bearded cadavers in decaying robes of green and black. He shut them again. "We're going to get in so much trouble," he said.

"From who, our parents? We'll be back in our beds before they even wake up. And not from the church. The doors are never locked here. They welcome people at all hours. Even whiny little fraidy-cats."

"I changed my mind. I want to go home. I don't want to meet Father Light."

Derek sighed. "What are you worried about? He's cool as hell. At least he's not going to goddamn molest you. That's the province of the Catholics, don't forget. His interest in us is the farthest thing from prurient."

Ray gave him a look.

"Oh Ray, what I'm saying is that he doesn't want to fuck us."

"Jesus, Derek, I knew what you meant. You just sound…"

"I sound like someone who's educated himself. You might want to pick up a book some time, even the ones they give us at school."

A loud chord of an organ sounded, causing both the boys to jump. Derek burst out laughing as the chords climbed, and the man in the cape came around from behind the altar to stand above them. Derek looked up at Father Light, smiling. The Father's broad mouth was open in a fanged grin, his nostrils flared. From the split skin at either side of his forehead curled a long and pointed horn. It was Derek's understanding that Father Light's appearance corresponded with what he who beheld him wanted to see. And indeed, to Derek, Father Light looked a good deal like Christopher Lee from the old Hammer films they played on Channel 38's Four O'clock Movie. Derek looked down at Ray, who once again had covered his eyes.

"Open your eyes, Ray-Ray," he said. "Tell me what the

Father looks like to you."

"There's nothing to be afraid of, my son," said Father Light. Derek loved his accent. It even sounded like Lee, full of portent, with a touch of the dramatic, melodramatic, even, with a hint of potential cruelty.

Ray opened his eyes, beheld Father Light. His eyes went wide, so wide it hurt. His hands went up to his mouth and a dark stain of urine spread across the front of his pants.

THE SEGMENTED MAN

He is jawless, lanky, a litany of gangrenous ledges and mold-strewn folds tucked into a suit of a particular vintage. An exquisitely wilted cravat. Goat-eye cufflinks gilded green. A watch on a chain, its arms whirling madly. Candy colors swirl in the sockets of his eyes. He opens the great doors of his ribcage and beckons you in. And you enter, all of you, into the cathedral of bone, where maggots in formalwear undulate on the parquet dancefloor, where insect clouds contract and expand in the gaseous blue heavens, where ruined oyster-flesh slides down a spine of marble. Insects click and chortle. Somewhere a hidden heart pumps purple blood through an endless labyrinth of corridors choked with moth-eaten garments. You cavort in suites of exquisite obscenity, slide down serrated bannisters, drink from cupped hands brackish juice, become both host and parasite. You metastasize though cells like cancer. You are the Segmented Man.

The Segmented Man slips down silent suburban streets in the pre-dawn chill.

The Segmented Man reclines face-down in liquefied cadavers.

The Segmented Man rides fungal spores up to the peeling-paint ceilings of forgotten mansions.

The Segmented Man licks ash from the walls of homes condemned by fire and smoke.

The Segmented Man's black dreams taint the milk of the Mothers of Leeds.

GRAVEYARD WORMS

Mickey and Jade lay at the far end of the cemetery adjacent to the campus, next to the ornate iron gate. Their hands moved under their winter coats, pushed their way past belts and down into denim and cotton. Clouds of white steam escaped their mouths and moved along their faces before dissipating into the cool air.

She ran her tongue along his bottom teeth, then pulled his tongue gently between her lips. He opened his eyes to look at her. He loved the view: her squeezed-shut eyes, her eyebrows up in passion, the light spray of freckles on her forehead, her long red hair fanned out in the grass. He kissed her neck, then behind her ear. Then he saw the worm. Pinkish purple, it made its way through her hair, pulsing, contracting slightly. He pulled his hand out from the back of her jeans and began to stroke her hair. Gently, cautiously, hoping not to alert her to what was happening, he extracted the worm. It was longer than he'd expected.

As he flung the worm away, he saw another one tangled in her hair, this one fat and wrinkled, darker in color. Then two more thin ones. Well, shit. She shifted beneath him, moved her hands up and down his hips, pulled him against her, hard. One after the other, slowly, gently, he pulled and flung, pulled and flung. Each time he thought he was done, he discovered another.

Finally it seemed as though he'd finished the job. He looked back at Jade's face. Her eyes were still squeezed shut – he could see that her eyeballs were moving under them, as though she'd fallen into REM sleep. But her hands were up under his jacket now, under his shirt, her nails lightly scratching his chest. She was moaning softly, with a smoker's rasp, though he didn't think she was a smoker.

He pushed both his hands up into her now worm-free hair, and then he gasped. The surface of her head was soft, yielding, like a crumpled eggshell. He pushed in slightly with his thumb and heard a grotesque squelching sound. A worm, long as an arm, smeared with blood, slithered out of the wound in her head and through his fingers as he watched, frozen in horror and disgust.

He moved to pull his hand from her hair, to recoil, but as he did the top of her head slid off and onto the grass, soft as pudding. Long, pulsing worms pushed out from under her eyelids, crowded out of her nostrils like tenants fleeing a collapsing apartment complex. Her jaw opened and slid to the ground, her tongue thumping in the grass, as he scrambled to his feet and ran.

The campus was alive with students and slow-moving cars, throngs of revelers revealed in headlight beams. Up the hill the lights from the football stadium pushed a column of illumination up through gathering fog. Mickey pushed his way through, throngs of students, all headed toward the stadium. It occurred to them that he heard no voices, though, only shuffling feet, the friction of jacket on jacket, underscored by the distant marching band music pumping out into the fog along with the light.

Turn around, he thought. See their faces. All is well. All will be well.

And so he turned, walking backwards now, seeing what bubbled above the necks of the crowd, in the caves of their hairdos. He laughed and laughed, and then reached up to dig at the top of his head, to free into the world his terrible and forbidden and monstrous thoughts.

ENCOUNTER WITH POPE SEVENIUS

They contacted you to do a walk-through of the squat little house that had appeared one day on a city block of shut-down factories and boarded-up tenement houses. They had seen your articles on the church desecration and the incidents on and around Prospect Avenue, and they trusted your commitment to accuracy and your avoidance of the exploitative and sensationalistic.

The structure stood not much taller than a man of medium height standing on the shoulders of a very tall man, serrated spikes sticking out on all sides among unevenly placed, amorphously shaped windows tinted red. Impaled on one spike was an unlucky sparrow. Its wings moved, either due to the light wind, or a vestige of life still remaining.

You were taken aback by the policeman who met you at the makeshift gate the city had erected around the structure. Something yellow crusted his mustache and it appeared as though he'd been crying. His dress blues were misbuttoned, his holster unlatched, service weapon nowhere to be seen. A fresh cut split his cheek, orange fat visible behind the bubbles of brown blood. He had a bright, enflamed rash along his mouth, or else was wearing garish red lipstick. He greeted you wordlessly, unlocked the gate, and walked slowly into the fog.

You circled the structure, as no entrance was evident. In the back, by the alley, you discovered it: two sets of adjacent staircases, quite steep, each sufficiently wide to accommodate a shod foot, leading up to an aperture just wide and tall enough to accommodate a man of average weight. When you approached, each staircase began to move up and down, independent of the other. You stepped on and managed to climb your way to the entrance above, knees aching by the time you get there.

When you attained the top you wriggled in, and then fell scrambling onto a fat mattress below. It smelled brand new. You rolled over and sat up, and there he was at the foot of the mattress, the mad Pope Sevenius, in robes depicting animated scenes of torture and infanticide, his hands upraised and cupped, a lump of excrement in each. His features were mercifully occulted behind gossamer red veils. He inverted his hands, letting the excrement fall to the floor, and then he gathered his robes and lifted them high. His crotch was a wicked face with a pushed-in nose and a wet, fanged mouth.

Then he turned and bent over. In the few artistic depictions you'd seen of the Pope, he'd had a tail. What you saw in the squat little structure that had popped up one day on a street of caved-in sidewalks and permanently caged storefronts was not exactly that, it was in fact a profoundly prolapsed anus that dangled to just above his knees, and those were not bruises that covered its surface, but lipstick kisses.

You turned away and read the graffiti on the wall as the Pope approached, walking backwards, humming a nasty tune.

what politicians don't want you to know. what jesus doesn't want you to see. what estheticians don't want you to touch. what phlebotomists don't want you to regurgitate. what dogcatchers don't want you to read. what foot fetishists don't want you to eat. what news anchors don't want you to see in the Motel 6 on Route 10 in Fortsworth at 11:30 p.m., Room 204

BAKER'S DOZEN

The morning is stark still and blue-gray. The stores are closed, the streets and sidewalks empty. The old men huddled at the donut shop counter fall strangely silent. The emergency lights blink in time with the stoplights outside, signaling no one knows what. Gary drops a coffee carafe despite hands sticky with liquid sugar. The carafe explodes, the cloud of glass and hot coffee slows and stops in the air. Someone flips the page of a newspaper and scoffs.

Clara chain smokes Marlboro Reds outside by the dumpster, reading the graffiti. Foxcroft was here. Satan Rules. There once was a girl named Dirty Meg … Alex Hearts Bonnie… Permilia is Easy….

The grass goes pink. Everything does. Clara looks up, squinting. Ax blades soar across a sky composed of interlocking red rotors, shooting off sparks like shattered lightning bolts. One spark lands next to a dirt-browned clump of snow at Clara's feet and she stomps it into the mud with her red Converse All-Star. She turns to go back in, her break having ended five minutes back. But someone has locked the door. She rolls her eyes, groans, and then trudges through the mud to the corner, but a shadow in the grass stops her cold. Someone is waiting, back to the wall, just where the sidewalk starts. The shadow elongates. Clara flicks the cigarette butt to the ground and turns to flee, but a long white hand grabs the hood of her sweatshirt. She struggles, but to no avail.

A siren starts to howl, and then stops short.

Gary, legs and stomach burned bright red and blistered under steaming khakis and polo shirt, finds Clara at the end of his shift when he's throwing out the uneaten crullers. Her head is split open above the eyebrows. Inside is a damp cluster of digital watches with plastic bands. When he turns her over, her head opens like a puppet's

91

mouth and they spill out onto the ground. They all read 3:07 a.m. Gary decides to go inside to call the police, but the back door is locked. He circles the building only to find the entrance locked as well. Through the window he sees the old men, now crowded behind the counter. They are grabbing donuts and shoving them into their mouths, their shirts caked in powder, jelly like gore smearing the corners of their mouths and running down onto their sweaters.

Gary bangs on the window. Something is walking up behind him, scraping the sidewalk. He can almost make it out in the reflection. His heart pounds with both fists on the cell doors of his ribcage. He bangs harder on the window. The old men look up. They point. Their eyes widen. Then they cover their mouths and look away. Long white hands cover Gary's eyes. They smell like embalming fluid and blood.

THE HIGHWAY PROCESSION

Kevin Behlmer walked loose-limbed and smeary-eyed along the shoulder of the highway. Dawn's light stained the horizon a gauzy violet. The air had that smell particular to pre-dawn winter days, sharply cold, bracing, clean. Kevin could not smell it. He was still drunk, and the odor of the beer that he'd spilled on his polo shirt filled his nostrils. In his right hand he held an empty brown beer bottle, grasping it tightly around its neck like a totem, that it might prolong his fading buzz and forestall the inevitable hangover.

No cars had passed. The groan of a faraway train was the only indication that anyone anywhere was awake, or even existed.

The night before returned to Kevin in flashes. A loud bar, you had to shout in order to be heard. A girl, blonde, with a bob cut and torn tights under denim shorts, her lips tasted like waxy strawberries. Carrie? Cassie? Cassie. Stumbling down the bar-lined street among the other college kids, an ecstatic camaraderie of intoxication, shouting and hailing one another with toothy grins, slaps on sweat-stained backs. A loft apartment fogged in blue cigarette smoke. Cassie again, or Cassandra, his hands under her shirt, sliding up her warm waist. Nothing after that, just smudged snapshots of Christmas lights and drink-blurred faces.

The groan of the train is louder now. Not a train, then. Something approaching on the road. At first Kevin sees it as an eighteen-wheeler with its lights out, slowly cresting the hill ahead. But no. It's a group of men, tall, with lank white hair. As they pass under a streetlight, he sees their faces, like turtles' faces, but bespectacled and whiskered. Their hands are massive and grey; thin, long fingers drag on the concrete. A casket rests atop their heads, brand new, unmarred, fresh from the showroom floor, it seems.

The men stop just yards from Kevin, who shivers now, the cold just starting to hit him. They kneel, the front-most men the lowest, and the casket slides down their heads to land on the surface of the highway. One of the men kneels and undoes the clasps.

A child clambers out of the casket, in blue pajamas with cartoon sharks swimming among coral reefs and grinning starfish. His hair stands up on end, and his mouth is curled into a frozen sob, his eyes wide and unfocused, wet and red from crying. He looks up and around at the towering men and begins to sob, to cry for Mommy. One of the men lifts him up and bites off his jaw, clean as you'd please, and flings the shock-slackened boy into the casket. Another set of small pink fingers curls up over the edge, but the tall men slam down the lid, sending four small pink fingertips tumbling down onto the highway.

Kevin is backing up slowly, smacked in the face sober. His breath flows out of him in great plumes. He'd had those same pajamas. That boy's face looked like his own. He reaches up to touch his jaw, but finds only his top teeth, the curved roof of his mouth. The great tall men seem to grow taller around him as he approaches the casket. He opens the lid as the men begin to sing, and he climbs in to comfort his sister.

THE STUFFED ANIMALS

As it was nearing midnight, a house meeting was in order, decided Patrick Fowler. While it need not necessarily be formal, he thought, he should at least put on his pajamas. He chose the grey and black checker pattern, buttoned it up neatly, making sure everything was even and straight.

He began to pull the committee members from the trunk. There was Little One, an accurately named small, short-legged dog with a denim hat and a tiny protruding tongue; Ritchie-Bear, a yellow Pooh knockoff with a blue shirt, shining black eyes, and an inverted triangle for a mouth; Devil Dog, a forlorn, floppy dachshund; Joey, a fat-legged, freckled boy in a striped shirt whose bowl-cut hair Patrick had over the years sucked into a towering dreadlock; and Earl the Squirrel, who was, despite his large size, oddly realistic-looking.

That should be it. But there was one more down there among the Lincoln Logs and the action figures and the winter hats. Had he forgotten about one? Sticking his tongue out of the corner of his mouth, Patrick reached down into the trunk to pull up the face-down figure of a man clad in black. It was stuck, somehow, so he pulled harder. It peeled off from the floor of the trunk with an unpleasant squelching sound. Patrick flipped over the doll and regarded it.

A barrel-chested man in a sewn-on tuxedo looked back at him with a face of molded plastic, mottled as though with acne scars. Its fixed black eyes glared from shadowed hollows topped with low, straight brows. Below a piggish nose its pink mouth curled unpleasantly downward. Sideburns—they felt real under Patrick's fingertips—jutted below his large ears, ears to which the thing's designer had apparently paid painstaking attention, down to the wiry black hairs and the copper-colored smear of earwax. It looked like some kind of perverted Nutcracker.

"What's your name?" said Patrick. "Mister White Nose? Noise! White Noise. You may join the meeting, but the first time around your vote doesn't count."

The small chairs and miniature were still out opposite his bed; he hadn't put them away after his last meeting. Lazy! He sat the convocation one-by-one in the chairs. He let Mr. White Noise sit on the floor with his legs under the table. He'd get him a chair for next time.

"So," said Patrick, once everyone was situated. "Who will take the minutes?"

Mr. White Noise raised his hand.

"Good idea, you can take them. I want them on my desk by…"

"Shouldn't Mom and Dad be here?" said Mr. White Noise. "And the baby? The baby should definitely be here."

Patrick shuddered. He hadn't put those words in the mouth of Mr. White Noise; the figure had spoken of its own volition. But he had spoken with authority, essentially made a demand in the form of a question. He had superseded Patrick's authority. A part of Patrick wanted to admonish Mr. White Noise, to have him physically removed from the meeting, but mostly he felt compelled to acquiesce. He rose and exited the room. "Stay here," he said, in a last-ditch effort to assert his authority, but his voice came out wobbly and weak.

21

THE ANIMALS, STUFFED

M om!" called Patrick, walking down the darkened hall. Shimmering light seeped onto the floor from the open bathroom door. Patrick went in. Candles guttered on the sills and the sink and on the back of the toilet. Mom was still in the tub full of red water, a large new mouth sliced just above her navel. A nest of purple snakes bobbed in the water, a green-handled kitchen knife tangled up in that nest. Mom's mouth was open in a grin so fierce her cheeks were torn. Her eyes were avid. The tips of her painted toes broke the surface of the water, little white islands with red cliff-faces.

"Family meeting," said Patrick. "I'll go get Dad."

He went downstairs to Dad's office. All of Dad was there, in the chair at the computer, all except his head. On the screen, large-eyed cartoon creatures cavorted, circling a lump of flesh that quivered on an altar. Jumpy organ music played. Dad clapped his hands brainlessly. The chair squeaked and squeaked.

Patrick left the room and went to the kitchen, opened the door to the microwave. Dad's head was there, just as he suspected it would be. His eyes were bubbling pools of white in the circular tray, his tongue out and split like an overcooked frankfurter. The hairs in his nose were singed. Patrick grabbled a couple of pot-holders and removed Dad's head, carried it up to the bedroom, and placed it on the dresser next to the radio. Then he turned and addressed the waiting crowd. "Mom should be here any second," he said, and as he said it, he heard dripping in the hall.

Mister White Noise rose from his chair and walked over to the dresser. He climbed up, little plastic hands gripping the drawer-pulls. When he attained the top, he briefly acknowledged Dad's head, and then switched on the radio. Static filled the room. Mister White Noise turned the volume all the way up and jumped back down, returned to his chair.

The door slammed open, revealing Mom in all her ripped-up glory. Little One's paws went up to his mouth. Ritchie Bear vomited up an impressive volume of shredded stuffing and fainted dead away. Devil Dog shook his head sadly. Earl the Squirrel twitched and bounced in his chair. Joey just stared at his phone.

"Let's get started," said Patrick, "for I'm told that a great storm is coming, and we must begin our preparations. We're going to need all hands on deck for this one."

THE ASH EATERS

Brandy didn't care much for Bryce's friends. It's not that they were outwardly unsavory; no, they were always smartly dressed, well-groomed, and polite, especially for eleven-year-olds. Maybe it was the politeness itself that was the issue. It seemed forced and false, like they were a little squadron of Eddies and Edwinas Haskell.

She'd pulled Bryce out of school for her father's funeral. When the old man had hit 88, he'd gone sour. Capriciously cruel and unthinking, quick to anger. Mean, even. So the death had been to some degree a relief. For now. She knew eventually that she would begin to recall the entirety of her life with him, of his life as a whole, the early part of it seen in old photographs and flickering home movies, his searing intelligence and his humor. His love for Bryce. But for now she knew only the welcome silence of his now empty sick room, and the silver, leaf-patterned urn on the mantle in the den, the urn that held his ashes, so small a vessel for such a larger-than-life man.

When he'd taken his last breath, Bryce was in the room. She was not. She'd run in at the sound of Bryce calling out, saw her father's gaping mouth and half-shut eyes, saw his final, merciful stillness. She'd knelt next to Bryce, whose expression was strangely neutral. "Bryce," she's said. "Pop is gone, son. Are you okay? Did he say anything?"

"No," looking up at her with those eyes. "He just tried hard to breathe a few times, and then he shook a little."

"Do you want to talk about death?" she said, hoping, with not a little guilt, that his answer would be No.

"Not yet," he'd said.

She arrived home, plastic grocery bags clutched in her hand. The television on the counter shone blue light into the darkened kitchen; on the screen a geeky, giddy weatherman pointed at a map dominated by a big blue blotch off to the east. An historic storm, he was saying. Epic proportions, he said, enunciating as though addressing children. Record breaking. Sure to be deadly. Politicians are issuing warnings. No such thing as essential personnel for this one, folks.

She walked to the counter, glanced to the den at her left, and dropped all the bags onto the floor. Bryce's friends were kneeling on the floor among the spilled ashes of her father, the urn upended, off to the side. They turned to her and grinned in unison. Their lips and tongues were caked with dust. One of them, a little girl, she thought maybe her name was Amber, sneezed, sending a billowing cloud of ash out in front of her. "Where's Bryce," Brandy said, and all at once she smelled the stinging odor of kerosene, felt the blossoming of searing heat at her ankles.

She looked down as flames shot up the legs of her pants, and she turned. Bryce was backing away, a little red cigarette lighter in his small hand. His whole face was covered in dust. He looked like a statue, she thought, as she fell to her knees and the flames immolated her blouse.

"Let's talk about death," said Bryce.

APOPTOSIS, OR THE DREAM OF THE RITUAL PIG

The office building, all white-framed windows and contoured glass, sits like a beached ocean-liner at the edge of the dead lake, among neglected landscaping and trees encased in dripping ice. Everything is still, anticipating the encroaching storm. The graffiti on the realtors' signs are as faded and illegible as the signs themselves. The interior is all hulking silhouettes lit dull red with EXIT signs. As dusk sinks from the sky, the security lights spit and sputter to life, illuminating snaking wires, cleared desks, rusted file cabinets, mold-splotched coffee carafes.

On the fourth floor, where at one time under punishing fluorescent bulbs a squadron of temporary workers moved virtual windows between dual-screens, a figure clad in rags and insulation and grey cubicle fabric emerges from a darkened hall into an expanse of carpet counterfeiting a leaf-strewn forest floor. His head is that of a great, decaying ancient hog, whose wild, rolling eyes and straining mouth suggest he is an unwilling participant, as does his horrible shrieking. He is as tall as the high ceiling, broad and thick-legged. In his swollen, mud-caked hands he pumps two bruised, lifeless cherubs with crepe-paper wings and protruding black tongues. The thing stomps and shrieks, squeezes the cherubs until their skin ruptures and their dead eyes bulge.

From behind the Hog comes a parade of women and men in suits stuffed with documents and memos; rude, splintered crucifixes impaling their heads, down through their tongues and out of their chins. Fat, feasting termites migrate from nostrils to eye-sockets to mouths. They form a circle around the Great Hog.

The Hog's shrieking abates and a silence falls over the assembled hierophants. It speaks in a high, nasal voice, the eyes still circling the room in terror and confusion. *The coming year is nigh upon us, and we summon the reign of frost, the plague of the milk-leech.* The workers pull clusters of paper from their collars and shake them in the air. *We tarry too long in black clouds of fear and of trepidation. I call on Pope Sevenius, imbiber of bile, master of flesh. I call on Gaap, Master of Mergers, who carries Men between Kingdoms. I call upon Mister White Noise, he who consumes all voices and vomits them into the airwaves.* The workers pile papers at the feet of the Hog, and set them alight with purple Bics.

The Hog ululates as the flames consume him, and the workers fall to their knees. They bang their chins on the floor, extracting the crucifixes. Their skulls collapse, go to milk. The flames rise. The windows burst. Night sweeps in on devils' wings.

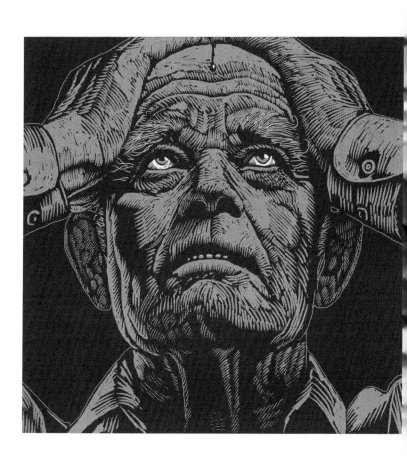

OUT IN THE STORM

The elderly man, clad in plaid pajama pants and an old t-shirt, wrapped in a bathrobe, stood on his front porch looking out at the snow-covered hedge, the rooftops and trees piled with snow. It was coming down fast now, heavy and dense, the air nearly as white as the ground. He stepped forward, out from under the overhang, and tested the snow with his slipper. Warm as a blanket.

He had been dreaming: In preparation for brain surgery, he'd taken the initiative to get a head-start. He'd used an X-ACTO crafting knife to cut a deep incision from the center of the back of his neck to just above the hair line. Then the phone rang – it was the doctor's secretary informing him that the surgery had been delayed indefinitely. For some unknown duration following the call, he kept having to push the halves of his head together because they kept separating. He awoke when he felt the contents of his head spill out and roll down between his shoulder blades.

The sudden revelation that he was alone in the house had frozen him in his chair. The subsequent fear that he was in the wrong house had driven him outside. It looked like his house, the clutter and the accumulated dust-gilded tchotchkes and knick-knacks and this-and-that and bric-a-brac, but he had been stricken by the sudden and sure certainty that it was a sham, a fraud, built up around him to make a fool of him. He had enemies. Just the sort of enemies who would do this to humiliate and shame him.

Somewhere, he was certain, somewhere near, was his real house. His family. He remembered a white-haired woman, curvy and lovely. She would bring him soup, yes, steaming and savory, made from scratch. He remembered a brown and white cat curled up like a cinnamon roll in a patch of sunlight. He remembered a dog with the saddest eyes, a dog who'd rest her head on the man's thigh and exhale as he stroked her impossibly soft ears. She's crawled up onto your shores, the woman would say. If the woman and the cat and the dog weren't here, they had to be at his real house.

He closed his eyes and opened them again to find himself on an unfamiliar sidewalk on an unfamiliar street, empty of cars and people, bereft of sound. The houses stood silent and white, windows darkened. Side streets split off, lines of two and three-story houses, all alarmingly close together, curving off into unknown neighborhoods. The nearest street sign read Goat's Path. He trudged forward, turned left onto that street. He closed his eyes again, for a long time, this time, until the sensation of being about to fall jerked him awake.

Now he stood downtown, the buildings like blind-eyed walls on either side of him. The snow was up to his knees now, and the cold hit him all at once. His mind flitted away to earlier times, when he was not quite young, but not quite middle aged. A house like a castle tower. A well-appointed study with a fire crackling and swaying behind an ornate grate. Walls of ancient books. Men in cowls kneeling on the floor in worship, and an upstairs hallway leading to many rooms filled with young women who would wordlessly open their pure and unblemished bodies to him. A lectern, him gripping it with red hands, delivering thundering speeches to a crowd who jostled and shoved to get a better view.

And then he'd met the white-haired woman, who was in those days a brown-haired woman, who had shared his dark vision. And the cat who looked at him with wisdom and strange knowledge in its kaleidoscopic eyes, and the dog whose affection was sweet and real and without guile.

His mind returned from its flight to find him seated on a curb. He felt over-warm. He shrugged his bathrobe from his shoulders. Somewhere under the snow he pushed off his slippers. Then she materialized from the snow, a twister of white flakes that formed a cloud that morphed into the shape of the white-haired woman. She offered him her breast and he turned his face up to meet it. He opened his mouth. The snow piled on his tongue and filled his throat. He heard the glorious chorus of a thousand frozen angels. He heard the beating of mighty hooves and knew that the wise cat and the sweet dog were near, were approaching. He pulled at the snow with his tongue, and he waited for the cloud inside him to burst.

The world ends every time a sentient being dies. Hundreds of thousands of apocalypses a day, piling up, metastasizing, a cancerous cloud that eats the world from the outside in and makes it clean.

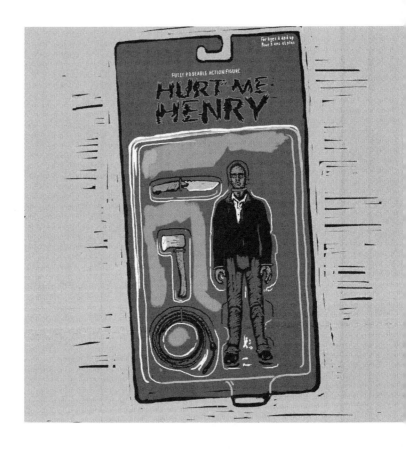

HURT ME HENRY

Sean snuck down the stairs. His parents had left the tree lights on, and the glow of the blues, reds, and greens on the white walls, heightened by the untouched white of the massive snowdrifts outside the picture window, lent the room an ethereal, fairy-tale aspect: a picture book Christmas morning. Gifts crowded the tree all around. One very big box stood out among the rest. He wondered what it could be. He reached for a small box just at the outer edge and had just peeled back a corner of the wrapping paper when the overhead light came on.

He gasped and turned around. His father stood in the doorway, hair standing up in all directions, black bathrobe tied taut around his waist, a steaming cup of cocoa in his hand. "Hey, boss," he said. "Getting an early start?"

"Yeah."

"Oh, that's okay, boss. I won't tell your mom. And she won't tell Dr. Rittle. And all will be well." He switched the light back off. "That's better, isn't it?"

Sean nodded.

"Well, you've gotten started on that one. Whyn'cha open it up?" He ambled over to the couch and fell backward onto it, holding his mug aloft to prevent overspill.

Sean pulled the wrapper off, revealing a slightly anxious looking doll of a man, trapped behind a see-thru plastic wall. Plastic ties held its ankles, wrists, and neck to the backing cardboard. HURT ME HENRY, the package read, in a red, ragged font. Henry wore a blue jacket over a white shirt, tan khakis, brown shoes. Adjacent to the doll, also lashed to the cardboard, were a miniature knife, hatchet, and whip.

"Ooh, Sean, Hurt Me Henry. That, if you didn't know, and even if you did, is just the most sought after thing right now. You have no idea what your dad had to go through to get that." He chuckled darkly. "No idea at all."

Sean tore off the plastic front, undid the twist-ties. He leaned the doll against a towering box, lined up the weapons next to it. Maybe it was a trick of the tree-lights, heightened by the still-falling snow outside, but the doll seemed to tremble, just slightly. "Hurt him, Sean," Father said, his voice slurring. "Stab him right in the gut."

Sean picked up the knife and poked at the belly of the doll. Father said, "Jesus Christ, kid. Did I raise a pussy? Did I? Stab him hard."

Sean thrust the knife into the belly of the doll. It groaned, and its hands flew to its sides. It slid down and curled into the fetal position, its eyeballs flying about madly in their sockets. Sean skittered backwards on his butt, saying "Oh shit, oh shit, oh shit."

Father cackled. "It's just a toy, kiddo. Just a doll. It's manufactured to do that."

"Dad," said Sean. "The rug! Mom's going to kill us!"

"Don't you worry about your mother, son. Hey. Hey. Let's try the hatchet. Cut off his hand."

Sean rolled the doll onto its back. A loop of rubber intestine dangled from the stomach wound. He picked up the hatchet, lifted it high, brought it down on the doll's wrist. The doll emitted an electronic shriek from the little speaker in its back as its hand rolled away twitching and little jets of blood shot out of its wrist. "No, no, Eric," its distorted voice called through a cloud of static. "Make him stop."

Sean whipped his head around, looked at Father, squinting.

Father put his mug down onto the carpet, put his elbows on his knees. He belched. "Take the whip, Sean." Pull down his pants and shove it right in his little plastic asshole. Don't. Hold. Back."

"Dad," Sean said. "Where's mom?"

"You know, Sean, that's a good question. That's a very good question. Hey. Hey. What do you suppose is in that big old box right there? What do you suppose? Why don't we open that one? Henry can wait." He stood. "Can't you, Henry?"

The doll whimpered.

Sean walked over to the big box. Fear tore through him. It felt very cold in the room. Very cold. The sun was beginning to rise. The houses across the way, not much more than rooftops and second stories peeking out from over the sweeping snowscape, were still and dark, backlit. Soon lights would come on, families would sit around their trees, laughing, opening gifts, getting exactly what they wanted. Sean tore down a swath of red and green striped wrapping paper.

Father walked over to Henry and positioned him just right, so he could see.

"Merry Christmas," Father said, as Sean slid the toy knife along the tape and the cardboard flaps opened. "Merry Christmas, darling."

ABOUT THE AUTHOR

Matthew M. Bartlett lives in Western Massachusetts with his wife Katie and their cats Phoebe, Peachpie, and Larry.

www.matthewmbartlett.com

ABOUT THE ARTIST

Yves Tourigny is a Canadian biped from the Ottawa-Gatineau region, Yves busies himself with game design and illustration. He does not plan to outlive his Chihuahua.

www.yvestourigny.com

Bizarre radio broadcasts luring dissolute souls into the dark woods of Western Massachusetts. Sinister old men in topcoats gathered at corners and in playgrounds. A long-dead sorcerer returning to obscene life in the form of an old buck goat. Welcome to Leeds, Massachusetts, where the drowned walk, where winged leeches blast angry static, where black magic casts a shadow over a cringing populace. You've tuned in to WXXT. The fracture in the stanchion. The drop of blood in your morning milk. The viper in the veins of the Pioneer Valley.

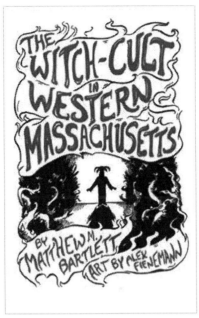

Meet Stanley Malanson, who had a curious rapport with felines. Meet Abrecan Geist, who endeavored to take revenge on a capricious God. Meet Minerva LaBrie, who abandoned Wicca in favor of a dark and blasphemous alternative. Meet Jebediah Blackstye, who crossed a line with his beloved familiar, a toad with revolting powers. These are but four of the practitioners of black magic who have made their homes in the cities and towns of Western Massachusetts. Read of sumptuous feasts gone to rot, of a corrupted priest who dared unleash his venomous platitudes over the common airwaves, of a powerful sorcerer born at the intersection of Blood and Stone. Open your hearts to the Witch-Cult in Western Massachusetts.

Matthew M Bartlett

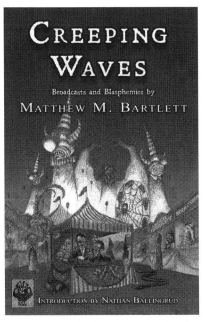

Where is the real Leeds? How does one get there? Is it floating on the air—words and music you can almost reach out and grab like wriggling worms of sound and ether? Is it in the carnival that seethes under the corrupted church, drawing the lost along shadowy corridors and through the strangely angled Funhouse doors to the place where the city fathers perform secret rites with the goat-headed masters of the dark? This is WXXT. It's the witching hour, when shadows take wing and nightmares stalk. Turn your radio up. Point your antennas to the infinite sky. And stay tuned for Weather on the Sixes. WXXT. The bubbling blisters on the tongue of the Pioneer Valley.

Five years prior to the publication of Gateways to Abomination, Matthew M. Bartlett put out a book called Dead Air. That book is now extremely scarce. This volume contains most of the unpublished work from that book, a few dark poems, and stories and fragments that later appeared in Gateways to Abomination and Creeping Waves. It also features magnificently creepy artwork by Yves Tourigny, as well as Tom Breen's original introduction. Witness the early days of dread magus Benjamin Stockton, and of his demonic radio station WXXT, with all its guts, worms, wriggling things, and voices from the dark.

Made in the USA
Middletown, DE
13 November 2018